HOORAY FOR
Hoppy!

For Keelan

First published 2014 by Macmillan Children's Books
This edition published 2016 by Macmillan Children's Books,
an imprint of Pan Macmillan,
20 New Wharf Road, London N1 9RR
Associated companies throughout the world
www.panmacmillan.com

ISBN: 978-1-4472-5709-7

9 8 7 6 5 4 3 2 1

A CIP catalogue record for this book is available from the British Library.

Printed in China

HOORAY FOR
Hoppy!

tim hopgood

MACMILLAN CHILDREN'S BOOKS

Hoppy woke up bright and early.
He wiggled his nose and sniffed the air.
Perhaps today's the day! he thought.

But as he hopped to the top of his
hole, he saw that the world was
covered in snow.

"Too cold," he said, and he hopped
back to bed.

The next morning, when Hoppy hopped to the top of his hole, his nose felt cold and the grass felt crunchy.

"Too icy," he said, and he hopped back to bed.

A few days later, Hoppy woke

up much earlier than usual.

Perhaps today's the day!

he thought.

Hoppy twitched his nose,

the air smelt fresh.

Perhaps today *really is* the day.

The day that spring arrives!

So Hoppy hopped down the hill

to see if it were true . . .

"Hooray!" said Hoppy, as he heard the birds singing.

"It **sounds** like spring has sprung."

"Hooray!" said Hoppy, as he sniffed the pretty flowers.

"It **smells** like spring has sprung."

"Hooray!" said Hoppy, as he watched

the lambs in the meadow.

"It **looks** like spring has sprung."

"Hooray!" said Hoppy, as he nibbled the fresh green grass.

"It **tastes** like spring has sprung."

"Hip hip hooray!" said Hoppy,

as his feet touched the warm ground.

"It even **feels** like spring has sprung."

Today really is the day! thought Hoppy.

He couldn't wait to see his friends.

But when he reached

the top of the hill . . .

. . . There was nobody there!

So he thumped his back feet as hard and
as loud as he possibly could . . .

"**Hooray!**" shouted all the rabbits,

as Hoppy leapt high in the air.

Spring had definitely and most wonderfully sprung!

There are five senses that we use to discover the world.

1 Hearing

We listen with our ears.
What can you hear?

What does Hoppy hear?

2 Smell

We smell with our noses.
What can you smell?

What does Hoppy smell?

3 Sight

We see with our eyes.
What can you see?

What does Hoppy see?

4 Taste

We taste with our tongues.
What can you taste?

What does Hoppy taste?

5 Touch

We feel with our hands and feet.
What can you feel?

What does Hoppy feel?